TEMPLE RUN

TAKE CONTROL OF THIS STORY IF YOU DARE

™

GET READY TO RUN FOR YOUR LIFE!

With special thanks to Adrian Bott.

EGMONT
We bring stories to life

First published in Great Britain 2015 by Egmont UK Limited
The Yellow Building, 1 Nicholas Road, London W11 4AN

Cover illustration by Jacopo Camagni
Inside illustrations by Artful Doodlers
Text & illustrations copyright © 2015 Imangi Studios, LLC

ISBN 978 1 4052 7634 4

www.ImangiStudios.com
www.Egmont.co.uk

59586/1

A CIP catalogue record for this title is available from the British Library.

Printed and bound in Great Britain by the CPI Group.

Stay safe online. Any website addresses listed in this book are correct at
the time of going to print. However, Egmont is not responsible for content
hosted by third parties. Please be aware that online content can be subject
to change and websites can contain content that is unsuitable for children.
We advise that all children are supervised when using the internet.

TEMPLE RUN

RUN FOR YOUR LIFE!

™

VOLCANO ISLAND

EGMONT

Like most kids, you always suspected you'd be famous some day. But you never thought you'd achieve fame by discovering an island from the comfort of your own bedroom!

You'd read about all the amazing things people had found by using Internet search engines to look at satellite pictures. Shipwrecks, lost Roman villas, ancient ruins buried in the forest — you could be an explorer without ever leaving your home! One person even thought they'd found Atlantis, but it was just a glitch. That didn't put you off. You just kept looking. One day, you told yourself, you'd find something the whole world would gasp at.

You were searching through satellite images one night, hovering over a blank bit of the Pacific Ocean, when you found something amazing. A whole island, not on any maps, with what looked like ruins all over it. You couldn't take your eyes off the orange dot in the middle. Could it be a volcano?

It turned out you'd rediscovered an island that everyone had thought was lost. It was believed to have disappeared beneath the waves centuries ago. Now here it was again, as if it had resurfaced from the sea, just waiting for you to find it. Could it be your destiny?

The story hit the headlines, and next thing you knew, internationally famous explorer Karma Lee was calling you on the phone. Karma was putting together an expedition to investigate the island. She had some experts she wanted to bring along, but the big question was, did you want to come too?

Well, DUH. Of *course* you wanted to come.

There are so many questions that still need answering. Why has the island reappeared? Why isn't it on any maps? How has it stayed hidden all these years? Most intriguing of all, is anyone living there?

★

You're on the way to the island without a name on a luxury ship, the *Ororo*. The weather's fantastic. A hot tropical sun blazes down over rolling blue waves. You sit on the deck eating tapas with your fellow passengers, learning more about them.

There's Karma Lee, who turns out to be just as friendly in person as she was on the phone. She's about to make some kind of announcement, and you can tell she's excited.

Barry Bones, the police officer, is more stern and serious. Despite being on a boat in the sunshine, he's not treating this as a holiday. He says he has a case to crack, but won't say any more just yet.

Then there's the red-haired Englishwoman, Scarlett Fox. She's all smiles, but you're not sure you can trust her. She's a bit *too* friendly, in the way people can be when they want something from you.

Later that evening, Karma gets everyone to gather around the table for her announcement. She brings out a little leatherbound journal that looks hundreds of years old.

'Many centuries ago, this account of the island's discovery was written. The author was a Chinese sailor whose ship was blown off course in a storm.'

'An ancestor of yours?' you ask.

'Yes. My own great-great-great-great-and-a-few-more-greats-besides-grandfather. His journal was taken from the island by his son, the only survivor of their fateful trip. It has been passed down from fathers to sons and from mothers to daughters. Now, at last, I can retrace his steps.'

'Wait,' you say. 'Your ancestor didn't make it off the island?'

Karma shakes her head. 'His son escaped. He did not, and there are no clues in his journal that suggest why. I mean to find out what happened to him.'

So Karma's going to find the last resting place of a guy who died centuries ago. That's a big ask, but it's cool too.

'So what does he say about the island?' Scarlett Fox is excited, but Barry Bones is just listening, calm-headed and thoughtful.

'It's like something out of a fantasy,' Karma admits. 'He describes a terrifying volcano goddess, and mentions some kind of lava temple, protected by "wicked beasts, like demonic monkeys of the underworld, and the monstrous Island Guardian".'

Scarlett's eyes grow wide. 'A temple?'

'I thought that might spark your interest,' Karma grins. 'I admit, the thought of a temple is intriguing to me too. Imagine what treasures might be found there. But most of all, I want to retrace the steps of my ancestor and find out what ultimately happened to him.'

Barry Bones nods. 'What about you, Miss Fox? What's your role here?'

'Oh, nothing very exciting,' Scarlett says, and you just know she's not telling the truth. 'I'm just a tech geek, to be honest. I'm coming along to make a geographical survey of the island using some advanced scientific instruments, and to investigate its weird electromagnetic field.'

'That's a lot of gobbledygook, Miss Fox, if you'll forgive me. Electromagnetic what-now?'

'Field. There have been lots of strange disappearances of ships and planes in this part of the world. I'm working on a theory that the magnetic field has something to do with it.'

Karma butts in: 'And you're here investigating one such disappearance, right, Officer?'

'As it happens, I am. I'm tracking the last known

whereabouts of Alfred Vanderbolt.'

You recognise that name right away. 'The bubblegum billionaire!'

'That's him. Built up a worldwide candy empire, then just abandoned it all.'

You search your memory. 'Wasn't there a crazy story about him flying off into the sunset with a plane full of gold?'

Officer Barry Bones nods slowly. 'That story is pretty much true. Including the part about the gold. Millions of dollars' worth of gold bullion were in the cargo hold of that plane. Enough to start a whole new life.'

Scarlett whistles softly. 'And you want to rescue him and his gleaming fortune. How public-spirited.'

Barry's voice is cold. 'Alfred Vanderbolt has responsibilities, Miss Fox. People depend on his candy business. Shopkeepers, factory workers, and millions of kids who just love his products. I mean to bring him home to them, if it is in my power to do so.'

'Land ho!' comes a cry from above.

'Well,' says Karma, 'here's where we find out the truth.'

You run out on to the deck for your first look at the mysterious island. Far in the distance, you see what can only be a volcano, surrounded by lush green vegetation. A column of smoke is rising from the volcano crater. The breeze blowing to you smells funny, like bad eggs.

'The volcano's active!' you say.

'Yeah,' says Scarlett. She looks rattled, not like her usual cool and collected self. 'My readings are showing dangerous levels. It's not only active, it could blow at any time.'

'So whatever we do on the island, we need to do quickly,' says Karma. 'Keep it tight out there, my friends. I haven't waited this long just to see all the island's secrets lost forever under a wave of lava.'

Next second, a flaming rock the size of a car comes hurtling through the air towards you. Is the volcano exploding already?

The sailors on the deck yell and dive for cover.

The rock splashes down just ahead of the ship, sending up a fountain of white spray. The ship rocks from side to side as the waves buffet it.

'That was too close!' gasps Karma.

A creepy feeling comes over you. It's as if something threw that rock at you on *purpose*.

The captain decides to anchor the ship a little further away from the shore, in case it happens again.

★

Y ou are on the deck of the *Ororo*, looking inland through a pair of binoculars. You get a good view of the whole island from here. The volcano rises high above the rest of the island, and you think you can see a path running up the side, like a spiral ramp made of platforms. At the foot of

the volcano are sprawling stone ruins. You glimpse statues and overgrown buildings.

'Those ruins are mentioned in the journal!' Karma tells you. 'See that dome? My ancestor calls that the Onion Tower. There's even a sketch! Oh, wow, this proves it. He really did come here, all those years ago.'

On the western side of the volcano is a long

stretch of jungle. You hear birds squawking and see animals moving among the foliage.

It's Barry Bones's turn to sound excited. 'I think I see something. Looks like a plane's wingtip, torn off, hanging in the trees.'

Scarlett shrugs. 'It doesn't look like plane debris to me.'

'Oh, and you're the expert? That's a crash site all right. Alfred Vanderbolt's on this island somewhere. Alive or dead, I'm going to find him.'

Scarlett points out a large group of huts in a bay, directly ahead, surrounded by a giant, reinforced wooden fence. 'Looks like some people made it here alive, at any rate.'

She's right. You focus the binoculars and see people moving in and out of the huts, people of all sorts of different races and ages. They can't be native to this island, surely? In fact, they're wearing the ragged remains of modern clothing.

There's only one explanation. 'They must be shipwreck survivors!' you say.

'From a lot of different ships,' agrees Scarlett. 'But look at that stockade they've built. Why do they need that? What danger could they be defending themselves against?'

'If that volcano erupts, they'll be toast,' Karma says quietly. 'Captain, can you bring the ship closer? Maybe we can give them a lift out of here.'

'Not possible,' the captain says. 'Another rock like the last one, and *plouf!* We would be stuck here too. You'll have to use the dinghies.'

Everyone agrees you need to head to shore right away. Scarlett Fox gives everyone a walkie-talkie. 'If we're going to split up, we need to stay in touch with one another. Check in on the hour, OK?'

'Roger that,' you tell her.

The question is, who do you go with?

Barry wants to go and look for the crashed plane in the jungle. 'I could use some help,' he tells you. 'You'd be doing a rich man a big favour, helping him get home.'

'I'm going to go talk to those people in the

stockade,' Scarlett says. 'They're all survivors. If anyone can explain what's caused the wrecks, they can. And I want to get them off this island.'

'That's a noble thing to do, but I still want to go to the ruins first,' Karma says. 'I need to find my ancestor's remains. I need to know what the great secret was that he couldn't bring himself to write down before his death. Want to come?'

To go with Barry Bones, head to page 14.

To go with Scarlett Fox, head to page 107.

To go with Karma Lee, head to page 67.

'I'll help Barry look for the crashed plane,' you say, decisively.

Exploring a dangerous jungle in search of a missing candy tycoon sounds like your kind of an adventure. Besides, just imagine how generous Alfred Vanderbolt might be to the people who rescued him! You think he could easily spare you a million or two, just to say thanks.

'OK. But be careful,' Karma warns you. 'There's something very strange about this island. I don't like the way that rock came flying straight for us. It's like something was trying to hit the ship.'

Barry puts on a pair of mirrored sunglasses. 'What do you think we'll find in there, Ms Lee? Rock-throwing dinosaurs?'

'There are more things in heaven and earth . . .' Karma starts to say, then stops herself. She shakes her head. 'Just be careful.'

The crew get the dinghy ready for you. You climb down the ladder on the side of the ship and step in. The dinghy wobbles under your weight.

Your walkie-talkie crackles. 'This is Karma. Check in, over.'

You have to laugh. 'Karma, we've not even left the ship yet. I can still see you.'

'I know. I just wanted to make sure you were OK.' She waves down from the deck. 'Good luck!'

You try to reply, but Barry starts the motor and the roar drowns out your words. You rush towards the island, sea spray flying in your face and a plume of white water in your wake. This is fantastic.

'We'll land the dinghy over there, on that spit of land,' Barry yells over the engine noise. He points to a golden beach jutting out on the edge of the jungle.

As you draw closer, you see a grey rock formation looming up out of the trees like the head of a stone giant. If you could get up there, you'd have a great view of that part of the island.

You're half way between the ship and the shore when you see something out of the corner of your eye. A dot, flying up out of the volcano, arching across the sky, growing bigger as it comes closer. You stare. It's another rock, bigger than the first. At first you think it's heading for the ship, but then . . .

'Barry!' you yell. 'That rock's going to hit *us*!'

Barry throws the little dinghy into a curve. White water flies up as he desperately tries to get you out of the path of the oncoming boulder. You can only hang on for dear life as it comes whistling down.

KRATHOOM! A wall of water wrenches the dinghy up and over like a toy boat. Suddenly you're floundering in the water, gasping, struggling

to swim. The world goes green, then blue, then green as your head goes under again and again.

By a stroke of luck, you grab the taut rubber side of the dinghy and hang on. Barry, his sunglasses gone, surfaces opposite you. Soaked, you both struggle back into the dinghy.

'That was *definitely* aimed at us,' you say.

'Yeah,' Barry answers darkly. 'I think that's a given. And we need to get to shore fast, or whoever's launching those rocks is going to sink us.'

Barry starts up the motor again. He steers the dinghy inland on a zig-zag course, in case more boulders come flying at you. Luckily, they don't, and the dinghy is soon crunching to a halt on the sand of the beach. The two of you pull it up and out of the water for safety.

'I just hope it's still here when we come back,' Barry says.

You look around, but you don't see anything dangerous nearby. Maybe wild creatures don't come to this jungle-infested part of the island.

Or maybe they're just really good at hiding.

'OK, we've got a choice. Where do you want to start looking?' says Barry.

You gaze at the jungle ahead of you. You can only guess at what might be lurking in there, among the creepers and tangled trees. That rock formation you saw is sticking up out of the trees a way away, and in the distance beyond that, towering over everything, is the smoking volcano.

You've got two options. You can head for the rock formation and try to climb up it. You'd get a great view of the land around you, and you might see Vanderbolt's crashed plane. But anything that was watching, like the mysterious rock-flinger, would probably get a good view of you, too.

Or you can head straight into the jungle and look for clues there, like pieces of the plane or even gold bars that might have fallen out of it. It'll be an effort hacking through these vines, and there might be savage creatures in there, but you'd be less of a target.

To head for the rock formation,
run straight to page 20.

To plunge into the jungle, go to page 22.

'Let's make for that rocky outcrop,' you say. Barry nods, pleased. 'Smart move. We'll be able to see for miles up there.'

You press onward into the jungle together. Every sudden sound makes you jump. You notice brightly coloured birds in the trees and strange blue beetles crawling on the jungle floor. You've never seen anything like them before, even on nature shows or in museums. This whole island seems like it's fallen through into your world from a different reality.

Soon, you see grey stone through the endless green forest. You've reached the rock formation! You frown as you notice how oddly shaped it is. It almost looks like a figure, hunched over.

Barry stops in his tracks. 'It's a monkey,' he says in awe. 'It's a statue of a dang monkey!'

He's right. This is no mere rock formation. It's a scary, gigantic statue of a monkey with a skull for a head. A flock of birds flies up, squawking. You suddenly don't feel too safe out here.

'It's not a *life-size* statue, right?' you hope out

loud, remembering Karma's ancestor's description of the beasts that once guarded the island.

'Come on,' Barry says firmly. 'Let's climb that thing. We've got a job to do.'

Just as you're about to follow him, you see an odd green shape waddle through the undergrowth. You can't resist having a closer look. It's a turtle, but its  shell looks *exactly* like half a melon. And it has the cutest little face!

'You coming?' Barry snaps.

He's being pretty uptight. Probably goes with the job, him being a cop and all. The turtle begins to trot away from you. You don't like to leave something so rare and adorable behind. Maybe you should try to catch it. It's bound to be an unknown species, and it could make you famous!

If you want to run after the melon turtle and try to grab it, head to page 24.

To run after Barry and climb up the statue, scramble to page 26.

The thick mass of jungle trees around you blocks out almost all the light. You step on something that wriggles, and quickly put your foot down somewhere else.

'Stay alert,' Barry warns, putting his back up against a tree for a moment and glancing around before moving on. He's acting like he's tailing a criminal through the city streets. You don't really think he knows much about jungle survival.

'What exactly are we looking out for?' you ask.

'Debris, and damage to the local area,' Barry says. 'If Vanderbolt's plane did crash here, it would have taken down a few trees . . .'

There's a soft *whup* noise. One moment Barry is talking to you, the next he's dangling upside down from a tree branch. There's a rope made from woven vines around his leg.

'Help!' he yells. 'I'm caught! It's some kind of a snare!'

You hear rustling from the trees around you. It might be whoever set the snare, coming back to investigate. Or it could just be wild animals. You're not sure if you can take the chance.

You could quickly hide. That way, if someone (or something) nasty is coming, you'll have the advantage of surprise. But that would mean leaving Barry helpless.

Or you could try to free Barry. But then you'd have your hands full when whoever or whatever it is comes and finds you here. Then it might get both of you instead of just one.

You'll have to choose fast!

To hide, go to page 29.

To free Barry right away, go to page 30.

You ignore Barry Bones's angry shouts. You *want* that melon turtle. In fact, maybe you should grab more than one. That way, you could raise a whole family of them back at home.

The melon turtle wobbles away from you, moving as fast as its stubby little legs can carry it. 'Get over here,' you mutter. You duck a tree branch, hop over a root and lunge for it like a footballer.

Got it! The turtle gives a loud squeak like a rubber toy and waggles its legs. You tuck it under your arm. It's making a lot of noise, but you aren't bothered. You have the best pet ever.

Now you'd better get back to Barry. You go to retrace your footsteps, but then you freeze. You hear the whirr of hundreds of pairs of wings. Little shiny shapes are shooting through the trees, darting around the branches, coming directly at you. They're not birds, nor bats. They look almost like fish!

The turtle squeaks again. More of the strange winged fishes come hurtling out of the shrubbery. One of them whizzes up to you and sinks sharp teeth into your leg. Ouch! You drop the turtle in shock and it trundles happily away.

All too late, you understand what's happened. These are winged pirahnas, and they were attracted to the turtle's frightened squeaks.

By the look of them, they were expecting a meal. Now they've got one. They seem happy. Their dinner tonight is going to be a LOT bigger than a melon turtle.

Unfortunately, this is the end of the road for you. At least you've made some hungry winged pirahnas very happy. They're a very rare species, you know. All but extinct in the rest of the world. You should feel good about helping keep them alive. Well, maybe not . . .

RUN AGAIN? TURN TO PAGE 10

The monkey statue is covered with tough vines, so it's easier to climb than it looked. You are soon standing on the monkey's shoulder, helping Barry up. He's out of breath.

'Go on up to the head, kid,' he gasps.

You scramble up on to the weathered stone skull and stand looking out over the island. Barry was right; you've got an excellent view from up here. You can see right over the wooden fence on the beach, to the huts where a ragged group of people are welcoming Scarlett Fox as if she were an angel of mercy sent from heaven.

You tell Barry about it. 'Good for her,' he says. 'With any luck, we can get those poor souls *and* Vanderbolt off the island. Of course, we've got to find him first.'

He's got a point. You remind yourself you're here to find Alfred Vanderbolt, if he's even alive. You shade your eyes and look carefully across the jungle for any sign of him.

Then you see it. The tailfin of a plane, jutting out

above the jungle trees. 'Barry!' you yell. 'I've found the plane!'

Barry excitedly passes you up a pair of binoculars. 'I knew it! Take a good look. Tell me everything you see!'

It's definitely Vanderbolt's light aircraft. The serial number matches. You make out the plane's fuselage, down among the greenery. It's dangling out over a steep drop above a river but it looks like it's not too badly smashed up. That means Vanderbolt could have survived.

You and Barry are in high spirits as you climb back down the statue. Unfortunately, the good mood doesn't last. There are three people waiting for you down at the bottom, wearing the tattered remains of clothes and carrying crude spears. They don't look at all happy!

There's a vine dangling from a tree close by. If you jumped and grabbed it, you could swing down, hit the ground running, and sprint for your life.

Then again, these people look like shipwreck survivors. They might just be suspicious of strangers. After all, it's bound to be a long time since they've seen any. You could try just talking to them and see what happens. The group at the stockade made Scarlett welcome, didn't they?

To swing from the vine and flee, go to page 73.

To talk to the savage-looking group, go to page 33.

Barry glares at you, but since he's dangling upside down from a tree, it doesn't look as scary as it might. You scurry away and crouch behind another tree, hoping you're well hidden. You peer through a jungle fern as whatever-it-is comes striding into the clearing.

It's a guy. A tall, tanned, bearded guy wearing shorts . . . and a crazy collection of weapons. He's got spears, a bow, what look like hand-carved boomerangs, and even some bolas. He looks at Barry and his hand goes to the knife at his waist. You hold your breath. A bead of sweat rolls down your forehead. What are you going to do?

To break cover and attack the hunter, go to page 37.

To stay hidden and see what happens next, head to page 39.

You pull out Barry's knife and almost fumble it in your haste to set him free. You start to slice through the rope, noticing how cleverly woven it is. Someone on this island is *really* good at making rope out of creepers.

'Hurry!' Barry hisses.

You mutter that you're going as fast as you can. The rope snaps all at once and Barry goes tumbling to the ground. As he picks himself up, you hear a chuckle from somewhere in the jungle nearby. You spin around and catch sight of a tall bearded man, deeply tanned and with a wild look in his eye. He's carrying a bow, but he's not pointing it at you.

'Amateurs,' he says. Then he turns and vanishes into the jungle.

'Wow. What was that all about?' you wonder.

'I think that guy was Vanderbolt!' Barry bursts out. 'But why didn't he stick around and talk to us? Doesn't he want to be rescued?'

'Who knows. This island is getting weirder by the minute,' you say.

'Well, whoever he is, he didn't leave in the direction of the huts by the beach. He's headed deeper into the jungle. We should get after him, fast!'

You grin at that. Barry's in Cop Mode again, tailing a suspect. Then an idea strikes you. 'But what if he's expecting us to follow him? He could be leading us into more traps.'

'That's a risk I'm willing to take,' Barry says. 'We can't lose him now.'

You aren't so sure. Next time it might be you with your leg in a trap – or your neck! It might be a better idea to go slowly and make sure you're safe.

To rush off in the direction Vanderbolt left in, like Barry wants to, head to page 89.

To go after him at your own pace, making sure you don't set off any more traps, go to page 42.

You take a deep breath and charge at the monster.

'Bad move!' it yells, in Karma's voice. 'I don't know what you are, you slimy two-headed creep, but if you want a fight, I'm your girl!'

Slimy two-headed *what?* Suddenly, you realise what's happening. The fumes from the volcano are making you and Karma see things! You think she's a snake monster, while she thinks you're some kind of double-headed swamp goblin. So *that*'s why this place is called the chamber of strange visions . . .

Unfortunately, by the time you figure out what's going on, Karma has counter-attacked. She kicks you so hard she knocks you out. Luckily, that brings her to her senses, and she's able to carry you back to the ship for emergency medical treatment. Your island adventure has come to an abrupt end!

RUN AGAIN? TURN TO PAGE **10**

You wave at the group. 'Hi, guys! Don't mind us. We're cool.'

The hunters – two men and a woman – look up at you. 'Get off that statue!' the woman says. 'Don't ask questions, just get down, quick!'

You wonder if you've upset them somehow. You and Barry scramble down and jump the last few feet on to the ground.

'This way,' the oldest hunter says, and leads you away from the statue. You follow the hunters through the jungle until you're completely lost. You just have to hope you can trust them.

Once the statue is out of sight, the hunters breathe a sigh of relief. 'I don't think we were followed,' the woman says. 'You two got lucky. I don't think you know *how* lucky.'

'The demon monkeys don't like it when people go near that statue,' explains the older hunter. He points up to the volcano. 'See, the statue's a likeness of their great-grandpappy. The Island Guardian. He lives up yonder.'

'And the last thing you want to do is get them angry with you,' says the woman with a shudder.

'They're bad enough already,' agrees the older guy.

'Wait,' you interrupt. 'Did you say "demon monkeys"? Seriously?'

He nods. 'Evil little critters with skull heads. Most of the time they're just annoying, but if they decide they have a grudge against you, they will chase you down. And they won't stop till they catch you.'

'Thanks for the help,' Barry says seriously, and you agree. You imagine what it must be like to have a group of those horrible skull-headed monkeys chasing after you. You hope you never have to find out.

Now you're out of danger, you have a chance to talk to the survivors about the island. They explain that the community here is made up of people who've all been shipwrecked, or washed up ashore years ago. The wrecks are no accident, as you'd begun to suspect.

'It's him that does it,' the old hunter scowls. 'The Island Guardian. A great big demon monkey, up there on the volcano mountain. Whenever he sees a ship come close, he throws rocks at it until he sinks it. He even brought down a plane once.'

Barry looks excited. 'I need to ask you, is this man one of your community? He would have come down with the plane.' He flashes a picture of Vanderbolt.

The hunters look at one another. 'Yeah, we know him. But he's crazy,' the woman says, not really wanting to talk. 'He thinks he's this great hunter, you know? Prince of the island! He lives in the jungle by himself. Doesn't want anything to do with us. We can't even go too deep into these parts because of all the snares and traps he's set.'

'You'd better come back to the stockade with us,' says the third hunter, a bit more firmly than you'd like. 'It's not safe out here.'

Barry starts to protest that you've got a job to do out here, when a leaping, scrambling, hopping tide of skull-headed monkeys comes crashing through the trees. They screech in shrill voices. It looks like they want to tear you to pieces!

'Run!' Barry yells, grabbing you. 'This is our chance!'

You need to get away from the monkeys, but how?

To follow Barry, who's running further into the jungle, head to page 61.

To follow the hunters back to their stockade, head to page 46.

You charge out of your hiding place and rush at the bearded guy. He reacts with blinding speed, reaching for the bolas at his waist and flinging them.

They're nothing but a set of three rocks tied together with twine, but Captain Beardy has clearly had a lot of practice. They whizz through the air and catch you around the legs. In less than a second, they whip around your ankles and entangle you completely. You fall to the ground, helpless.

Beard-man sneers down at you. 'I was going to help you two out, but I've had second thoughts. You can stay here and rot for all I care. Have fun with the "wildlife".' He slips out of the clearing, leaving both you and Barry tangled up.

You spend the next few minutes frantically trying to get free of the bolas. Just as you loosen the last knot, you hear a hiss.

A long, scaly shape is writhing through the undergrowth towards you. You turn to run, but before you can move you see *two* snake heads launching themselves at you. Two fanged mouths bite deep.

Congratulations! You have just had the very, very rare experience of being bitten by a Gemini Snake! It's a bit of a shame that this means you've died a painful death, but at least you went out in an exciting and unusual way.

What do you mean, that doesn't make it any better? Well, if that's how you feel, you can always have another go!

RUN AGAIN? TURN TO PAGE 10

The hunter cuts through the rope. Barry falls with a painful-sounding thump. 'Ow! Careful, mister!'

'You'd rather I left you up there?' The hunter peers into the brush, looking right at you. 'Come on out.'

You hesitate.

'You're in no danger. Not from me, anyway,' the hunter says.

Warily, you step into the clearing. Barry disentangles the vines from his feet. The hunter suddenly looks off into the jungle. 'We need to move. They've got your scent.'

'Who do you mean by "they"?' you ask.

'You'll find out soon enough. Look, you two had better come back to my place. You'll be safer there.' Something about the hunter seems funny to you. He looks scruffy and wild, but he's really well-spoken, like some high-class college kid.

'What do you think?' Barry asks you. 'Do we go with this guy, or do we look for Vanderbolt?'

You put two and two together. 'Barry . . . I think we just *found* Vanderbolt.'

Barry stares at the hunter. The man doesn't turn around, but you hear him sigh. 'I should have known people would come looking for me. Come on. We've got a lot to talk about.'

Vanderbolt leads you past deadly traps in the jungle, where strange non-human skeletons dangle from the branches, to the safety of his hut. You settle down for a drink and a chat.

Go to page 47.

No sooner do you open the smaller door than several tonnes of rock fall down on you. You're very slim all of a sudden. In fact, you're flat. Like a pancake.

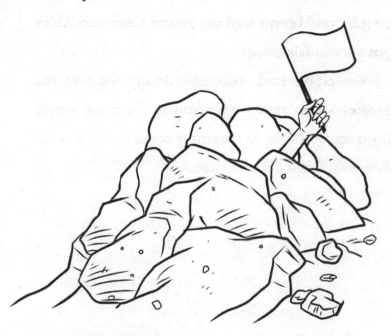

RUN AGAIN? TURN TO PAGE **10**

As you walk, a blast of heat hits you in the face. You notice the plants here are dried-up and lifeless, as if they'd been baked where they stood.

A few steps later, you find the reason. There's a river flowing at your feet, but it's not a river of water. It's a sluggish, glowing river of molten lava! To your right, the land slopes sharply upward, forming a rocky shelf overhanging the river. To your left, it slopes down in the direction of the sea.

Barry points upstream to the slopes of the volcano. 'The lava's flowing out of one of the vents, see? This island is more unstable than we thought!'

Which way did Vanderbolt go? The lava river is too wide to jump. He must have run across the toppled-over tree that's bridging the river a little way down. The tree is more of a scorched log, actually, now you look. The heat from the lava has blackened it.

Barry grabs your arm. 'Up there on the ledge overlooking the lava river. See it? It's the plane!'

He's right. The remains of Vanderbolt's plane are

dangling over the drop. Now you have to decide whether to go after the man himself, or explore the crash site. There could still be gold bullion in that plane, remember!

The only way to follow Vanderbolt now is over that scorched tree trunk.

To run out across it, head to page 117.

To climb up the slope to the clifftop and explore the plane wreckage, head to page 61.

Unfortunately, Scarlett was wrong. There isn't enough air in the dinghy to reach the ship. Before you're even half way there, it's just a flat rubber rag. The two of you are left treading water in the open sea.

As you flounder about, Scarlett tries to cheer you up. 'So we lost our dinghy,' she gasps, 'and now we need to swim to the ship. Look on the bright side. Things can't get any worse!'

You glance up and see a boulder flying towards you from the volcano. It looks like things are about to get a LOT worse.

'Oh, no,' Scarlett moans. 'Why did I have to open my big mouth?'

RUN AGAIN? TURN TO PAGE **10**

Even if it hadn't been a ridiculously long swim back to your ship, had you forgotten about the enormous rocks being launched into the water?

You don't even make it half way! At least you've made the Island Guardian chucking the boulders happy. Hitting a swimming kid from this distance first time is worth a LOT of points in the game he's been playing with himself all these years.

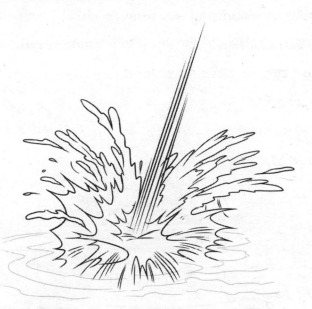

RUN AGAIN? TURN TO PAGE 10

You arrive at the survivors' stockade just in time to hear some terrible news. A boulder has hit your ship dead on, and it's sunk. You won't be going home for a long, long time.

Oh well. At least the islanders turned out to be friendly. You soon get bored of coconuts for every meal, and the crazy species of wildlife infesting the place are hard to live with, but on the plus side, you'll be able to go surfing any time you like! There are far worse fates than ending up on a sunny island.

RUN AGAIN? TURN TO PAGE **10**

Over a nice half-coconut full of fermented juice, Vanderbolt tells his story.

'When I ran away from my candy business to start a new life, I figured I'd settle in Hawaii, maybe, or Indonesia. I never expected to crash on this island during the storm. But it's the best thing that could have happened to me.'

'Best thing?' Barry asks. 'This I gotta hear.'

'I've never felt so alive!' Vanderbolt says. 'Back in the city, I was like a prisoner in a golden cage. I had everything I could ever want, so nothing mattered. Can you imagine how boring life is when a man can't think of a single thing he wants?'

'Must have been awful for you,' says Barry sarcastically.

Vanderbolt turns to you instead. 'Out here, in this savage world, I'm the real me. I fight for every meal. I run, I swim, I climb trees. I live like Mother Nature meant people to live.'

'Isn't it dangerous, though?' you ask, thinking of all the traps.

'It's dangerous as all heck,' grins Vanderbolt. 'There are these crazy little skull–headed critters everywhere you go – demon monkeys, I call them. But we've come to an understanding. They leave me alone, mostly, and I leave them alone. I'm the only one on this island who's earned their respect.'

As you listen to Vanderbolt talk, you realise he's happier than he ever was back home. It seems he doesn't want to go back to civilisation ever again. But Barry has come a long way to fetch him back. This is going to be a problem.

'Sir, I get that you're on some kind of natural living kick out here, but you have to come back with us,' Barry says. He stands up and moves to the door.

'I don't see how you're going to make me,' Vanderbolt says, narrowing his eyes. You tense. Is there going to be a fight?

'I'm hoping you'll see reason.' Barry's voice is dead calm. 'This island is dangerous. Fine, you don't care about your safety. But what about the kids?'

'What kids?'

'The kids across the world who love your candy, of course. They all wanna taste the new Vanderbolt creations. You got responsibilities, sir. You can't just turn your back on them!'

Vanderbolt's quiet for a long time.

Then, to your surprise, he turns to you. 'What do *you* reckon?'

He thinks that you, as a kid, will understand why he wants to stay here. Who wouldn't run away and live in freedom, if they had the choice? When Vanderbolt was a boy, he always loved to play in the woods, building camps and living off the land. Being rich and successful never measured up to that. Living on this island is hard, but he's free.

If you think Vanderbolt should come back to civilisation, head to page 58.

If you think he should stay here on the island where he seems to be happy, go to page 143.

'Follow me, and do exactly what I do,' Barry whispers.

Crouching low, he sidles up to the silent hut. There's still no sign of life from inside. He beckons you over and the two of you press your backs up against the log wall.

Barry explains, using gestures and mouthing, that he wants you to peer around the corner and see if there's a window in the back wall. You do. There is.

Barry lifts you on to his shoulders so that you'll be able to look through the window. Then, as quietly as he can, he steps around to the back of the house. Something underfoot goes *crack*. The next thing you know, you're falling.

You and Barry tumble through a convincing covering of jungle brush into a deep, earth-smelling pit beneath the house. Barry's fall is broken by the ground. Your fall is broken by Barry.

After checking to make sure you haven't fractured anything, you look around. There's no way out. There's some smoked meat hanging on a spear, though, and a full waterskin.

Vanderbolt appears at the lip of the pit and looks down at you scornfully. 'I haven't survived this long in the jungle by being careless,' he says. 'I expect my guests to be more polite.'

'Please let us out!' you say.

'In time. But first, you can cool off in my cellar for a while. Maybe it'll teach you some manners.' Chuckling to himself, he strolls away.

By the time Vanderbolt lets you out, a miserable-sounding Scarlett tells you over the walkie-talkie that a boulder from the volcano has sunk your ship. You're stuck here, and you've just managed to annoy your new neighbour, too! Things couldn't be *much* worse, but at least you're alive.

RUN AGAIN? TURN TO PAGE **10**

52

Vanderbolt answers the door as if you'd been paying a friendly visit back in civilisation.

'Oh dear. I wasn't expecting company. If I'd known you were coming I'd have baked a cake.'

'May we come in?' you ask. 'It's pretty dangerous out here.'

'Of course. I appreciate the respect you've shown by being polite.'

Vanderbolt invites you in to talk things through. Head to page 47.

But you don't make it to the dinghy. A swarm of skull-headed monkeys comes scampering down from the branches overhead. They snap their teeth at you, swipe with their claws and even pelt you with coconuts. Only a swift dodge saves you from a nasty whack on the head.

'Run!' Barry shouts. 'There's too many of them!'

He's right. You could handle one demon monkey, or two, but this horde of the things is just plain scary. They chase you through the jungle all the way down to the beach, and even then they keep coming.

'Do you think they'll chase us into the water?' you gasp.

'Let's not find out!' Barry gasps back. 'Look up ahead. There's a sea cave in that cliff, see it?'

'Got it.' You think it'll be easier to make a fighting stand in a cave than keep on running like this.

You and Barry scramble into the cool shadows of the cave. Already you feel safer. Especially since the monkeys don't follow you in. In fact they're keeping their distance. Strange . . .

'Help me move . . . some of these . . . rocks,' Barry says, fighting for breath. 'We'll block off the cave mouth.'

A wave breaks on the shore. Foaming sea water rushes into the cave, drenching your feet. The monkeys jump up and down and laugh at you.

'What's so funny?' you wonder.

Barry furiously hurls his rock at the demon monkeys, who dodge out of the way. 'The tide's coming in and this cave is flooding!' he rages. 'No wonder they wouldn't follow us in. They're just going to watch us drown.'

You're not going to give any demon monkey that satisfaction. You quickly think over your options. The demon monkeys don't seem to like water and they might not follow you into the sea. You could sprint past them and try to swim for your ship.

Or you could head into the back of the sea cave and try to find another way out of here. You know that sea caves sometimes have vents leading to the surface. But if you get stuck, there'll be no escape from the rising tide . . .

To try to swim to your ship, even though it's a long way away, wade to page 45.

To explore the darkness at the very back of the cave, which could be hazardous with no light, head to page 62.

B arry cautiously steps on to the plane. He yells excitedly that the gold is still there, only to howl in terror as the plane starts to give way and slip down into the chasm. You grab his arm and help pull

 him to safety just in time. The plane and the gold go tumbling down into the lava many feet below, lost forever.

As if things couldn't get any worse, you hear the ominous scampering of many pairs of animal feet approaching. Sounds like they're coming for you! Barry suggests you beat a retreat. You flee back towards the beach in the hope of reaching your dinghy.

Head to page 53.

The plane creaks and shifts under your weight as you climb on board. There's a note here from Vanderbolt! It begins 'To whom it may concern . . .' It explains how he's determined to start a new life here in the jungle. Now you know he survived the crash.

You see a gold bar, thrown loose from the others, gleaming on the plane floor. So that part of the story was definitely true! Your heart skips a beat as you see a set of boxes at the back of the plane. That must be the rest of the gold.

To grab the single gold bar and leave, go to page 64.

To try to grab a box full of gold bars, head to page 124.

Vanderbolt agrees to return to civilisation with you, if a little reluctantly. He accompanies you and Barry back to the ship, much to the Captain's relief, as the rocks are starting to fall much too close for comfort. Barry calls Scarlett and Karma back to the ship too, explaining that police business has to take priority. He promises you can come back to the island and help the shipwreck survivors soon.

'You took a big risk, coming to find me,' Vanderbolt says. 'I guess I owe you for that.'

'You're welcome,' you tell him.

'Hey, I don't suppose you've got any gum on you? That's one thing I did miss, living in the jungle. When I was a kid, making my camps and treehouses in the woods, I always had a pack of bubblegum with me. It's what gave me the idea to start the company.'

Luckily, you've got some gum stashed in your back pocket. You give him a piece. A huge smile spreads over his face as he chews.

'Now, what can I trade you for this?' he says. 'Hmmm . . . this should do it.' He reaches into his back pocket and passes you something about the size of a candy bar. Except it's heavy. And shiny. And golden.

You gasp. He winks. 'Better hide that, or they'll all want one.'

You quickly tuck your solid gold ingot away. Vanderbolt strolls off down the deck, whistling to himself.

As you sail away, you wonder if you've done the right thing. What if the island vanishes again, like it has done many times before, and you're never able to find your way back to it? If only you could have discovered more of the island's secrets . . .

RUN AGAIN? TURN TO PAGE 10

The only way out of here is across the roofs of the temple complex. The corridors have already filled up with molten lava. You run, jump and run again, skidding and nearly flying off the roof altogether, while the giant monkey pursues you. His foot goes right through the roof of one building, and you manage to scramble away while he struggles to free himself.

You're in danger of running out of rooftops here. Up ahead, you can see a river of lava crossing your path, flowing through the smashed remains of a building. You could leap over it and keep going, jumping from rooftop to rooftop, or you could do something daring and crazy and quite possibly brilliant. There's a stone dish nearby. You could grab it and try to use it as a surfboard to ride down the lava stream to the beach.

To keep going across the rooftops and risk running out of buildings, head to page 144.

To surf down the lava stream and risk being baked alive, head to page 148.

You and Barry run up the slope, gasping for breath in the heat. Jungle plants slap their fat leaves in your face and creepers draggle through your hair.

You stagger to a halt as you see a long, white shape looming through the undergrowth. You've found Vanderbolt's plane! OK, so it's dangling half off a cliff and only a few rocks are keeping it from falling all the way in to the boiling river of lava flowing below, but let's not spoil the party!

Either you or Barry will have to get on to that plane and look around. The gold bullion might still be on board! You're smaller and lighter, but Barry is tough and experienced. Which is it to be?

To let Barry go, head to page 56.

To go on yourself, head to page 57.

As more seawater comes washing into the cave, you wade through to the dark hollows at the back. Your phone shines enough of a light to see by – just.

The cave goes back much further than you first thought. It looks like it might go all the way under the cliff. The bad news is, it gets a lot narrower too. You manage to squeeze through, but Barry can't follow you.

'Don't worry about me, kid,' he says. 'I'll hold the fort here while you go on ahead.'

'But what about the demon monkeys? And the tide coming in?'

'Let me worry about that. Just get out of here!'

It's a wrench to leave Barry alone like this, but you don't think you have a choice. At least you can stay in touch with the walkie-talkie.

You press yourself through the tight gap and keep going. It's dark for a long time.

Then you feel hot air blowing in your face and see a dim orange light coming from somewhere in the distance. Is that . . . lava? The rocks are starting to feel warm, too.

You press on through the tiny crawlspace and keep on going, up and up and up, until you reach an astonishing room. From the look of it, you have to be in a sacred temple of some kind . . .

Continue to page 133.

Gold bar in your hand, you leap from the plane, just as it crashes away down the cliff, plunging into the lava, lost forever.

'That was *too* close!' Barry says as he helps you to your feet.

You try to give Barry the gold bar, but he shakes his head. 'You earned it, kid. You took the risk. Just make sure you keep it safe when we get home, OK?'

You can hardly believe it. You take another look at the gold ingot, gleaming bright as a buttercup in the sun. It must be worth a fortune. And it's *yours*.

A call comes through from Karma: you need to get off the island right away. It looks like the volcano's starting to erupt! You dash back to the beach and narrowly make it off the island before a huge cloud of smoke belches up into the sky.

The captain quickly steers the ship away. You realise you'll probably never know what became of the people on the island. Did they survive this eruption? Could you have brought them on to your ship if you'd had more time? At least you have a dazzling gold bar to remind you of your adventure. Perhaps you could use it to fund a return trip to the island . . .

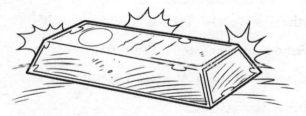

RUN AGAIN? TURN TO PAGE **10**

Your heart pounds as you desperately try to quench the flames. Your throat hurts from breathing in the smoke. You pour your whole bucket of seawater over the blackening timbers. Steam gushes up in a choking cloud, but there are still flames leaping inside the wooden frame. You just didn't have enough water to put it out. You turn to flee, knowing you can't possibly make it.

Suddenly Scarlett comes running, bringing a slopping-over bucket. She hurls the water past you and into the heart of the flames. With a hiss, they vanish and only smoke and mist remain.

'Good timing,' you gasp. 'I was nearly barbecued there.'

'I have my moments,' smiles Scarlett.

You hear Hawk bellow triumphantly. 'They've given up! They took their best shot and it wasn't enough. The monkeys are running!'

Victory is yours!

Head triumphantly to page 129.

Y ou and Karma Lee land your dinghy at the east side of the island, intending to explore the abandoned ruins at the foot of the volcano. The architecture's like nothing you've ever seen, a sort of hybrid of Egyptian and Mayan styles. This must once have been a bustling city, or a temple complex. Most of the stone buildings are still standing.

You stifle a yell as you notice that creepy, skull-headed monkeys are watching you from the rooftops. Those things are weird looking, but they don't make a move . . . for now.

Karma points out two ways you could go. You could head for the largest building, which her ancestor called the Gatehouse of Evil Gods. It leads into the ruins and divides them from the rest of the island. The gates are open right now, probably left that way hundreds of years ago when Karma's ancestor's son fled from here.

Alternatively, you could make for a dark opening a little further along the slope, which looks like it goes underground. Karma says that leads

to the Chamber of Strange Visions, whatever that is. Neither option sounds like it's going to be easy!

What's it to be?

To set out for the gatehouse, go to page 69.

To run to the underground opening, head to page 71.

The moment you start running, the monkeys screech and come at you. You dive inside the gatehouse with them close on your heels.

There are tall statues in this room, all with hideous faces. They must be the evil gods that Karma's ancestor wrote about. The stone ceiling above you, held up by slender pillars, looks really unstable. This whole building seems about to collapse. Further in, the rest of the temple complex looks a little sturdier.

'Close the gates!' yells Karma. 'Hurry, before those demon monkey things get their claws on us!'

You hesitate before doing what Karma says. You could close the gates and hope that's enough to keep the horde of demon monkeys out. Or you could ask her to help you topple one of the statues into one of the wonky pillars and try to bring the whole place down.

Closing the gates would be quicker and safer, but it might not stop the demon monkeys. Then again, collapsing the ceiling will leave you with no way out, and you might get buried alive.

To shut the gates, go to page 140.

To collapse the ceiling, go to page 80.

The skull-headed monkeys watch from a distance as you and Karma climb down into the tunnel. Some of them are hunched over and shaking in a peculiar way. You get the nasty feeling they're laughing at you. Weird. What do they know that you don't?

Karma wrinkles her nose. 'Smells bad down here. Fumes from the volcano, I guess.'

You wish you had a breathing mask. You and Karma switch on your torches to see a stone corridor covered with frightening, crazy carvings. Figures with bulging eyes and grinning mouths full of teeth seem to lunge at you. They're very lifelike!

'Maybe we should have gone through the gatehouse,' you mutter. But Karma doesn't say anything. She just coughs. The air down here is *really* stuffy.

As you move further down the corridor, you begin to see the carvings on the walls moving. The figures snap their jaws and clutch their claws at you. You turn to ask Karma if she's seeing this, but to your

horror, Karma is gone. In her place is a nightmare —
a half-human, half-snake woman with hair made of
hissing snakes!

If you want to be brave and attack the
monster, head to page 32.

To run away from it as fast as you can,
rush over to page 74.

Or you could always try speaking to it. It's
good to talk, right?! Go to page 142.

With a wild jungle cry, you launch yourself from the monkey statue and grab hold of the creeper, ready to swing through the trees. With an even wilder jungle cry, you hurtle towards the ground as the creeper breaks free in your hand. The group of islanders stare at you as you crash down into the foliage like the world's least successful bungee jumper.

AAAIIIIAAAAAAHHHH!

Fortunately, you're not dead. Oh, you've broken a few bones, but the islanders take pity on you and carry you back to their huts so you can rest and heal.

Head to page 46.

You sprint down the corridor, fighting for breath. Where on earth can Karma have gone? Did that freaky snake-woman swallow her whole? And why are the carvings still writhing around like a really cheesy special effect from a low-budget movie?

At the end of the corridor is a tomb-like chamber. There are skeletons standing upright against the walls, grinning at you. Their hands start to twitch. You really hope they don't come to life and start attacking you. It wouldn't usually seem likely, but right now, you're not exactly sure of what's real and what's not!

You feel a cool breeze from a crack down one wall. Fresh air! You run over to it and breathe in the cool, sweet, clean air. Your head begins to clear and the walls stop throbbing. Could the volcano's fumes have been messing with your mind?

Karma Lee appears in the doorway. She stares wildly at you. 'Who are you? What have you done with my friend? And why have you got two heads, you big ugly goblin?'

Oh dear. It seems Karma's still got a head full of poisonous fumes. She's getting ready to aim one of those lethal kicks at you. You need to decide what to do about that!

To tell her to breathe in some of the fresh air, head to page 77.

To flee down a sloping passageway and keep on running, head to page 151.

You swing the idol at the demon monkey as it launches itself towards you. It connects – but to your horror, the creature clings on and pulls the idol out of your grasp. It runs straight up to the Island Guardian and hands it to him, reverently. The Guardian turns away, chuckling to himself, and begins the long climb back up to the mountain temple.

You're so annoyed you forget to keep running. Before you know it a swarm of demon monkeys surges around you. You're hoisted above their heads

and they start carrying you away. You don't know where they're taking you, but it's not going to be for a slap-up meal and a well-earned rest. GULP.

RUN AGAIN? TURN TO PAGE 10

Together, you and Karma take deep breaths from the clean air source until your heads stop spinning and you both look normal to one another again. You decide against heading for the sloping passage leading out of here, since the fumes seem even stronger down there.

Karma figures out that the space behind the crack must be a tunnel to the upper ruins. Between you, you manage to widen the crack far enough to slip through.

Head to page 87.

You grin, knowing you can trust Barry Bones, and throw the idol as hard as you can. Barry catches it and runs away like a linebacker. The giant demon monkey runs furiously after him, but Barry is faster. While he keeps the Island Guardian distracted, you help evacuate the survivors.

Head to page 150.

Your timing is perfect. You ride the collapsing platform right to the edge of the tower balcony, then hurl yourself through the air. You land on the rough stone, get to your feet and run around to the doorway leading inside the tower.

Suddenly the whole tower shakes as the Island Guardian launches himself at it and crashes into the balcony. He wants that idol back, badly. Unfortunately, the impact rocks the tower to its already shaky foundations, and with the volcano's eruption already making the earth unsteady, it's just too much. Slowly but surely, the tower topples like a demolished factory chimney. Both you and the huge demon monkey fall down into the ruins.

The good news is that everyone else is able to get off the island, so well done there! You're a hero. But unfortunately you won't be around to celebrate. And you were so close, too!

RUN AGAIN? TURN TO PAGE 10

You shove the statue as hard as you can, and Karma gives it a mighty kick for good measure. It falls into the pillar, smashing it to pieces. A deep groaning noise comes from the ceiling above you, growing louder and louder.

The demon monkeys barge into the room, hissing and growling. You and Karma barely get out of the gatehouse before the ceiling comes crashing down on them. Many of the demon monkeys are buried in the avalanche of rubble.

'We're stuck here now, for better or worse,' Karma says, 'Let's move on before they dig themselves out!'

You head through the gatehouse and into the corridors and rooms of the main temple complex. Looking at the carvings on the walls, you are able to reconstruct an image of the kind of civilisation that existed here. The island's original inhabitants seemed to live in fear of two great terrors, the goddess of the volcano and the beast who guarded her treasure. The goddess is portrayed as a woman with hair made of flame, while the 'beast' is a huge monkey with a skull for a head. He looks strangely familiar.

'But look at the size of him,' Karma points out. 'See the little demon monkeys at his feet? He must be their god, or maybe their ancestor.'

You reach a long room where the ugly faces of carved monsters scowl down at you from the walls. Some have beaks, others long snouts, but they all look mean.

Half way down the room's length, a stone bridge leads across a flowing river of lava. Well, 'bridge' would be one word for it. 'Half-collapsed stone arch that looks like a child could push it over' would be a bit more accurate.

Karma consults her ancestor's journal. 'We have to cross the lava river. It's the only way through into the inner temple.'

'Cross over that?' you ask.

'My ancestor did.'

'It doesn't look strong enough to cross. Maybe it was back in the past, but not now! Couldn't we jump over the lava?'

'I might, if I had enough of a run-up. A one in ten chance, maybe. But you couldn't, no way.'

A distant rattle tells you that some of the buried demon monkeys are digging their way out, and are coming in your direction. You need to move!

Karma insists you go over the bridge, because that's what the journal says. You think you could throw a rope up and over an ugly looking carving, and then swing across instead. It would be dangerous, but then that bridge looks downright unsafe too.

To cross the bridge on foot despite your misgivings, head to page 83.

To try to catch one of the monster carvings with a loop of rope and swing across, head to page 85.

'OK,' you tell Karma. 'We'll do it your way.'

You offer to go first, since you're lighter than she is. You hold out your arms for balance and take the first step on to the bridge. So far so good.

'Careful,' Karma warns you. 'Don't rush.'

'I wasn't planning on it!' you mutter through clenched teeth.

Step by step, inch by inch, you edge out on to the bridge. You try not to look down at the lava, but you can't stop yourself. It gloops and bubbles. There are floating patches of wrinkly crust, like elephant skin. The heat coming off it is almost unbearable.

You're half way across now. So far so good. You take another step, feeling like everything's going to collapse under you any moment.

Next second, it does. The middle section of the bridge is suddenly gone. Stone blocks fall and plop into the lava, sending up gouts of molten burning rock. You go plunging towards it as well, too startled even to scream.

Karma moves blindingly fast. She leaps through the air in a soaring arc and catches you. Her arms wrap around your waist. You both land with a painful thump on the far side.

'A one in ten chance?' you ask her as you get to your feet.

'One always was my lucky number,' Karma grins. You move on, knowing the monkeys will have a much harder time following you now the bridge is gone. But there's no way back now, either . . .

Head to page 87.

'Sorry, Karma, but I'm not crossing that bridge for any money,' you tell her. 'I've got a better idea. Lend me your rope.'

Karma unfastens her climbing rope and throws it over to you. There are more scraping and digging sounds in the distance. 'Whatever you've got in mind,' she says, 'make it fast.'

You quickly tie a lasso, pick out a long-nosed carving that looks like a crocodile with indigestion, and toss the rope up. You snag the ugly carving first time. *That's a good omen*, you think to yourself.

You climb up on to a fallen block of stone. Swinging across the lava river should be easy peasy, lemon squeezy. What could go wrong? The rope looks sturdy and you've got plenty of room.

You give the rope a tug, just to make sure it's secure . . .

You pull the carving right out of the

wall. It must have been looser than it looked! It falls, along with the block next to it, then half a dozen more blocks, then most of the ceiling. You dive for cover as the whole far end of the room caves in.

'You seem to be pulling this ancient ruin down around your ears very efficiently!' yells Karma. 'Ever considered a career in archaeology? Or perhaps demolition?'

When the roar of falling masonry subsides, you can see the result of your handiwork: a pile of debris filling up most of the lava trench and reaching up to the now broken ceiling of the chamber. You can see a whole new set of rooms up there!

A falling block has smashed the bridge – well, you weren't planning on crossing it anyway. And the exit you were going to take is now blocked with rubble. There's nowhere to go but up. You and Karma scramble on to the pile of rubble and head up to the floor above.

Go to page 99.

You head down the stately ruined corridors of the temple complex. The scratching claws of demon monkeys resound all around you.

'Sounds like they're in the walls,' Karma says with a shudder.

Up ahead, you see a gateway filled with roaring flames. The image of a phoenix has been carved above it. You also spot a small door that leads off to one side.

Karma consults her journal for clues. 'Only those who are walking in darkness shall pass through the Phoenix Gate,' she reads. 'Any idea what that means? We don't exactly have that much time to figure it out.'

You remember the scratching of the demon monkeys in the walls and nod your head. You glance at the small door. Perhaps you could avoid having to solve the riddle at all and head through that instead?

But if someone's gone to the trouble of guarding this gateway with flames, there's got to be something immense behind it, you figure. Maybe it's worth taking a little time to think this riddle through.

To head for the small door, go to page 41.

To take some time to think, head to page 90.

Y ou and Barry find yourselves outside an expertly built cabin made from the trunks of jungle trees. The walls and roof bristle with whittled spikes. You can't see any traps, but that doesn't mean there aren't any. Isn't there a saying: the trap you don't find is the one that gets you?

'The person who built this place knows about survival,' you tell Barry. 'We should be careful where we step.'

Barry nods. 'Maybe we shouldn't go up to the front door.'

'Why?'

'Because that's what he'd expect us to do. Let's sneak around the back.'

You think about what do do next. Knocking on the door would be polite, and would show you've got nothing to hide. But a stealthy approach might be safer.

To sneak around the back, head to page 50.

To knock on the front door, go to page 52.

There must be a trick to this.

You think about what Karma read in the journal and wonder if that might be the key. Could it have something to do with closing your eyes as you walk through?

Or maybe you just need to time it right. You notice that the flames do flicker every now and then. But you would have to run through as fast as you can – the flickering lasts a matter of milliseconds each time.

To wait until the flames flicker, then make a dash for it, head to page 125.

To close your eyes and walk slowly through the flames, head to page 91.

Or you could still think better of it and head to the small door instead. Go to page 41.

Karma cries out a warning as you close your eyes and step into the flames, but it's too late. You take one step, then another . . .

Nothing happens. You're fine! The flames didn't even singe you.

'You shut your eyes, so you were "walking in darkness"!' Karma says, sounding impressed. 'So that's how it's done!'

She shuts her eyes like you did and walks through the Phoenix Gate too.

Head to page 93.

The watchtower crashes down and takes you with it. It's a pretty uncomfortable way to go. Let's just pretend it didn't happen, and end this part of the story with a lovely scene of you, the demon monkeys and the survivors all toasting marshmallows over the fire. There, that's nicer, isn't it?

RUN AGAIN? TURN TO PAGE **10**

'This is it! The gateway to the Inner Sanctum!' Karma shines her torch into the domed hall in front of you. Its beam lights up two huge double doors made from bronze, a pair of gigantic pillars holding up the ceiling, images of demon monkeys chasing people across the walls . . . and a skeleton, sprawled on the floor. You hear Karma's breath catch in her throat.

'Is that . . . ?'

'My ancestor,' she says. She bows her head in silence for a moment. You do the same, to show respect. Karma gives you a look of thanks.

Together, you approach the skeleton, and you notice something that amazes you. 'He's wearing armour. And there's a sword in his hand!' The bony fingers are still clenched around the lacquered hilt.

'See these little pots, with the fuses in?' Karma points to them. 'They're grenades. Clay jars full of gunpowder. One of the great Chinese inventions.'

'So this guy wasn't just exploring. He was prepared for a battle.'

The hairs on the back of your neck prickle. Karma's ancestor must have been determined to face the guardian beast in single combat, like a warrior hero! That explains why he sent his son away with his journal – so that the boy could escape, even if he perished.

Karma says, 'I'm so proud of him. He tried to save the island, and the lives of others, all those years ago.'

'I just wish he could have made it out alive.'

'Me too. But I'm honoured to be the one to take him home at last.'

You decide to leave Karma alone for a moment, so she can gather up her ancestor's bones in peace.

You walk up the steps and look at the bronze double doors. You reach out to touch them and snatch your hand away – they're hot! They must lead to the very heart of the temple, the lair of the Island Guardian . . . and, according to the journal, the place where some kind of priceless treasure is kept.

You're pretty sure the beast – which if the paintings on the walls are anything to go by is definitely a gigantic demon monkey — can't possibly be alive after so many hundreds of years. Then again, you can hear what might be the scraping of huge claws coming from inside, and the sound of something huge moving about . . .

If you choose, you can open the doors and go inside, though Karma won't follow you this time. She says she has to take her ancestor's remains back to the ship first. Since every route out of here is either barred, blocked or collapsed, she says she'll have to *make* a way out somehow.

To head straight into the temple's heart on your own in search of the treasures within, go to page 133.

To help Karma find her way out of the ruins and back to the ship, head to page 96.

'I'm sticking with you, Karma,' you say. 'We'll get out of this place somehow.'

She gives you a grateful hug. 'I wonder . . . what would my ancestor do?'

An idea comes to you. 'Hey, remember those pots of gunpowder? Do you think they'd still explode?'

'That's brilliant!' Karma's suddenly excited. She checks the powder. 'Still dry. OK. Stand back. This is going to be loud.'

You take cover behind one of the pillars as Karma stacks the gunpowder pots in a hollow in the wall, then lays a long trail of powder to act as a fuse. She lights it, and a hissing spark gradually creeps along the floor towards the pile.

You glance back down the way you came. No demon monkeys in sight. Perhaps you've escaped them at last.

Karma covers her ears. You quickly do the same. Next second, there's a flash and a roar. The ancient bombs still pack a punch; they make a hole big enough to drive a truck through. You can see blue sky outside.

'There's our way out of here. Let's go.'

Karma stops short. Demon monkeys are peering in through the hole she blew in the wall.

'Ready to fight?' she asks you without turning around.

You take a breath. 'Let's party.'

With her ancestor's sword in hand and his bones in a sack, Karma charges the demon monkeys and scatters them. You back her up, pulling demon monkeys off her and flinging them away down the side of the temple. Together, you scramble down the outside of the building.

After a harrowing run, the two of you make it to the beach and from there to the ship. The captain refuses to stay another minute.

You feel glad to have helped Karma on her quest. You go to join her at the railing and look back at the island in the distance.

Karma excitedly tells you that she's been looking through the possessions she found with her ancestor's body. Among them are several very interesting ancient scrolls. It seems one of them might be the clue to locating a treasure fleet that sank without trace hundreds of years ago.

'You were such an asset to me on this adventure,' Karma says, an excited little smile creeping on to her face. 'How would you feel about joining me on another one in a month or so?'

You would love to go exploring with Karma again. 'Why wait?' you say, grinning, and turn to the captain. 'Set sail for adventure!'

RUN AGAIN? TURN TO PAGE **10**

You clamber up the fallen debris and pull yourself on to the floor of a circular room. The light in here comes from multicoloured flames jetting from bronze nozzles in the walls. You can't feel any heat coming off them. That's weird.

You notice your arm is covered in gooseflesh. Behind you, Karma makes a *brrr* sound. 'My hair's standing on end. Like static electricity.'

'So's mine!' you tell her. You're sure there's a source of great power in this room, something mysterious and ancient.

'I've got the oddest feeling I've been here before,' Karma says, looking around. 'You getting that, too?'

'Yeah. It's like time isn't running properly here.' You remember Scarlett talking about an electromagnetic field all across the island that played havoc with scientific instruments. Maybe this room is where it's coming from!

Karma whistles. 'Check this out!'

She beckons you over to a doorway in the wall. At least, that's what it looks like. Then you realise it's just the shape of a door, carved into the rock. The smooth stone in the middle is wobbling and shimmering, like the air over a toaster when it's turned on.

Curiosity gets the better of you. You poke at it with a finger. Next moment, a tremendous force sucks you into the stone doorway and straight through it. With a yell, you're flung out on the other side.

Your surprise at having passed through solid rock is nothing compared to the astonishment you feel when you see where you've landed.

You're in what must be the central temple room. At one end, where a wall should be, there's an opening on to the core of the volcano. You can see the boiling lava leaping up in bursts. But that's not what takes your breath away. Nor is the enormous demon monkey looming over you, three times the height of a man. And it's not the golden idol on the plinth in the centre of the room either.

What really blows your mind is this: the temple

all around you is *intact*. The statues look as good as new. There's no sign of the ruin you were standing in moments ago. It's as if you've travelled hundreds of years into the past.

Then you see the proof. A Chinese man in full armour, carrying a sword, pushes open the bronze doors and strides into the temple. He sees the Island Guardian and stands in a fighting stance. Then he sees you and his eyes widen in amazement.

That's Karma's ancestor, you think. You've been thrown back into the past to the very moment when he confronted the demon monkey!

You bow to Karma's ancestor. He returns the bow. A thought comes to you. Perhaps you can stand as his ally in the coming fight! Perhaps history can be rewritten.

But then you look behind you and see the time portal is starting to close. If you ran for it with all your strength, you might reach it, but you'd be abandoning a heroic man to his fate.

To help Karma's ancestor fight the Island Guardian, head to page 103.

To flee back through the time portal before it shuts, head to page 106.

As you prepare to go into battle as a sidekick to Karma's noble ancestor, you see the time portal vanish behind you. You're stuck in the past forever.

But that's OK. You made your choice. Now you just have to hope it was the right one.

The Island Guardian bellows his challenge. You and the warrior let out a battle cry and charge.

The fight that follows is truly epic. It's so epic that people write poems about it and draw scenes on the walls of the temple in years to come. Swords flash, spectacular martial arts combos are pulled off, punches and kicks fly, and at the end of it all, the Guardian lies defeated. The unconscious monster is dragged away, to be bricked up in a stone prison where he can do no more harm to anyone. You are more than just an explorer now. You're a hero of the people.

With the fall of the demon monkey tyrant, the

island and all of its inhabitants are safe. Karma's ancestor survives the battle and becomes your firm friend. However, because he lives, this means he never sends his son away with his journal, meaning that Karma Lee never receives it, meaning that the whole expedition never happened in the first place.

That's the bad news. You've changed the entire course of history and created a major time paradox in the process.

At the end of the day, though, who cares? Karma's ancestor is a cool guy, his family welcome you into their fold, and you have plenty of awesome adventures. There are far worse places to end up, and far worse fates than becoming a legendary warrior hero!

RUN AGAIN? TURN TO PAGE **10**

You sprint back to the time portal. Karma Lee's ancestor will just have to fend for himself. You feel a little bad about this, but then you already know he's going to fail, because you've seen his bones.

You couldn't have changed history, could you?

You'll never know.

As you fall back through the time portal and go flying out of the other side, you make a horrible discovery. The room you're falling into is flooded with red-hot lava. You're coming out of the portal at some point in the island's future. It's a time when the volcano has already erupted! At least there's no sign of Karma Lee, so you have to hope she made it out of here somehow.

That thought is small comfort to you as you go plunging into the lava. It's a competent dive, with several nicely turned somersaults, but the landing is frankly amateurish and you lose points for the screaming. Six out of ten.

RUN AGAIN? TURN TO PAGE 10

You and Scarlett pilot your dinghy ashore, landing as close to the colony of people as you can get. Their home is a circular wooden stockade made from logs with sharpened ends, enclosing a group of shabby-looking huts. A tall watchtower overlooks the whole camp.

'Not much of a tropical paradise,' Scarlett says.

Someone up in the watchtower yells, 'They made it! Let them in, quick! The demon monkeys are coming!'

You and Scarlett trade glances. 'Demon monkeys?' you say together.

The stockade's gate opens from inside. 'Hurry!' screams a raggedy survivor.

You and Scarlett waste no time getting inside. People crowd around you, some of them weeping with joy that a rescue party has finally found them, others grim-faced for reasons they soon make you aware of.

They seem friendly and they make you welcome, tell you that their life is deeply dangerous. Their leader is a guy called Hawk, whose arms are covered in tattoos. He used to be a ship's cook.

Hawk explains to you how his ship was wrecked here a couple of months ago. He and his fellow passengers joined up with the survivors from other wrecks and crashes, and they've been struggling along ever since.

'The demon monkeys are the worst part,' says Hawk. He takes you up on to the platform that runs

around the inside of the wall. He points out black-furred creatures squatting on the rocks, with long claws and heads like skulls. You're flabbergasted at the sight of them.

'Most of the time they just throw coconuts at us. It's like a game to them,' Hawk continues. 'But if you go outside the fort, they'll try to eat you.'

'How do you live?' Scarlett asks, horrified.

'We manage, just about. We only ever go out

in groups, for safety. Fishing and hunting gets us enough to stay alive, if we're lucky.'

'And if you're unlucky?' you ask.

'The monkeys drive us back empty-handed.'

Scarlett takes you aside. 'We have to help these people! We can't leave them here like this. It's inhuman!'

'Yeah, let's help,' you say. 'But how?'

'There's enough room for all of them to escape on our ship . . .'

Hawk overhears and interrupts. 'We had ships too, miss. They got sunk. And if you bring yours any closer, it'll get sunk too.'

'The flaming rocks that come out of the volcano?' you ask.

'You got it. He might not hit you the first time, but he'll keep on until he does.'

You're about to ask who 'he' is when Scarlett says, 'So we ferry people over to the ship in the dinghy. That'd work.'

Hawk shakes his head. 'You'd save a few of us,

sure. But every time you take a batch over, there'll be fewer and fewer people left to defend the stockade. Those demon monkeys are smart. They'll swarm over the walls and eat whoever's left.'

'Fine!' explodes Scarlett. 'I'll . . . I'll . . .'

Before Scarlett can formulate a new plan, a voice screams, 'Demon monkey attack!' A coconut whizzes past your head and explodes on a hut wall.

'Everyone to your places!' roars Hawk.

You look out over the stockade. The demon monkeys have surged forwards and are hurling coconuts over the walls. Groups of them have surrounded the little fort on all sides. Only the beach is clear.

Scarlett says, 'Come on! We need to go and get the ship right this second. If this is the kind of life these people are leading, under constant attack from demon monkeys, then they deserve to be rescued straight away.'

'What about the flying rocks?' you ask.

'I don't care what Hawk thinks. Or that the

captain doesn't want to bring the ship any closer. I'm an excellent helmswoman. I can steer the ship myself if necessary. I'll make sure we dodge any rocks that come flying at us.'

She's got a point. You're not convinced, though. 'Wouldn't it be a better idea to help the survivors defend their stockade first and fetch the ship once the demon monkeys are driven back?'

Scarlett yells, 'They're used to fighting these monsters and you're not! The sensible thing to do is bring the ship closer. Let's move!'

To run back to the dinghy and go and fetch the ship, go to page 113.

To help the survivors defend the stockade, go to page 115.

'OK, Scarlett. I just hope you can dodge those rocks.'

'Just watch me,' Scarlett says.

You call out to Hawk: 'We'll be right back with the ship. I promise.'

Hawk lets you out of the gate quickly. 'I truly hope so, but your friend seems a little too confident, if you ask me. Good luck.'

'Thanks. You too.'

The stockade gate slams shut behind you. One of the demon monkeys notices you're leaving and starts to lope down the beach in your direction.

'Come on!' Scarlett leads the way as you sprint back to the dinghy. More of the demon monkeys are following now.

Pushing the dinghy out to sea, you wade into the surf.

Cold water washes over your legs. You scramble into the rubbery craft and start the motor. Luckily, it starts first time.

Scarlett climbs in next to you. 'Go go GO!'

You give it full throttle. You're pulling away from the shore when one of the demon monkeys gives an evil chuckle and flings a sharp spear at you. It misses you, but sticks into the dinghy.

There's a pop and a soft hiss of escaping air. 'We've been holed!' you yell.

'It's only little!' Scarlett insists. 'We can still make it back to the ship. Just keep going!'

Your dinghy is losing air at a frightening rate. You think you could definitely make it back to the beach if you turned around now. You might get all the way to the ship, but you'll be in all sorts of trouble if you don't.

To abandon your plan to fetch the ship and rejoin the survivors instead, go to page 115.

To keep going, head to page 44.

The settlement is under siege by the demon monkeys! All around you, people are yelling and running for cover. Coconuts come hurtling over the walls, and to your horror you see that some of them are on fire.

'They dip 'em in burning tar,' Hawk tells you. 'Cute, huh?'

'What can Scarlett and I do to help?' you ask him.

'Lending a hand? That's the spirit! Well, there are three things you could do. It's up to you.'

As you run through the camp, ducking out of the way of incoming coconuts, Hawk explains your options.

You could join the fire warden team. Your job there would be to grab buckets of seawater and look for buildings the demon monkeys have set on fire, then put out the flames before they get any worse. You'd need to be quick, alert and brave.

Alternatively you could help to man the wall defences. That means forcing back any monkeys who try to their hardest to climb the walls and get inside the stockade. You'd be right in the firing line if you took that job, so you'd need to be good at dodging flying coconuts.

Or you could head up into the watchtower and act as a lookout. Your job would be to keep track of where the monkeys are going and shout directions to the survivors, so they can go where they're most needed. You'd better not be afraid of heights if you want this job.

'What do you think, Scarlett?' you ask.

'You choose,' she says. 'Whatever you pick, I'll be by your side. These people need our help.'

To choose fire warden duty, go to page 118.

To join the crew on the walls, go to page 120.

To climb the watchtower and help organise the defence, head to page 122.

The tree trunk turns out to be more thoroughly scorched than you thought. You're half way across when it breaks in half with a terrible *crash*. Plunging into boiling lava isn't good for the skin, you know. It isn't good for the hair, either. Or the bones. Or anything, really . . . You're toast.

RUN AGAIN? TURN TO PAGE **10**

'We'll be fire wardens,' you say.

'Great,' says Hawk. 'Buckets are down yonder. Get to it!'

You're not sure how the demon monkeys are able to fling flaming missiles over the stockade wall without hurting themselves, but those coconuts are a heck of a hazard. You and Scarlett spend the next ten minutes running back and forth chucking bucketfuls of sea water over the burning huts inside the stockade.

It's hard work, but you can tell you're making a difference, and the survivors are grateful. These people don't have much in life, but you've managed to save what little they have from being burned to a cinder.

'I don't believe it,' Scarlett says. 'The demon monkeys are falling back. We're winning!'

'Don't jinx it,' growls Hawk.

Right on cue, a huge fireball soars over the stockade and crashes down on the watchtower. It looks like several coconuts stuck together. The demon monkeys must have worked hard on that one.

Flames go shooting up the sides of the tower. By chance, you're right next to it. You're the only person in the whole camp who can stop the fire. Unfortunately, it may already be too late. It looks like the whole tower is about to collapse on top of you!

You have a choice, and you need to make it quickly: do you try to put out the fire at the risk of being squished, or do you run out of the way as fast as your little legs will carry you?

To try to douse the flames, head to page 66.

To run away, head to page 92.

If you weren't fighting for your lives, this might almost be fun! The demon monkeys throw  coconuts at you, you throw coconuts at them, and every so often one of your side or one of theirs is knocked senseless. You manage to dodge every missile that comes your way. You even shove a monkey backwards off the wall. It lands on its rear end with a satisfying *thump*.

The demon monkeys throw everything they've got at you (literally) but your side still won't give up. Hawk yells, 'We're winning! Keep it up, guys!'

Just as it looks like you've got them beaten, you see a demon monkey getting ready to fling a big flaming missile right at the watchtower. If that thing hits, it'll bring the whole tower down in flames.

Should you risk a shot of your own in return? You look around to ask Hawk for advice, but he's busy wrestling a particularly stubborn demon monkey off the wall with Scarlett. Nobody else is nearby to help. It's all down to you now.

You've got one chance to bullseye the missile thrower with a coconut. It could save the day, but if you miss, you know that critter will be angry and it'll come straight back at you!

To fling the coconut and hope for the best, head to page 126.

To run through the camp yelling a warning instead, head to page 92.

You climb up to the lookout post on the watchtower. Scarlett passes you some binoculars.

From up here you can clearly see what the demon monkeys are doing. As if you were playing a video game, you get to arrange the defences. You shout down to the survivors: 'We need fire wardens by the gate! Big demon monkey coming in from the left side! More ammo to the walls!'

Everyone does as you say. You're a natural leader. Scarlett backs you up, pointing out sneaky demon monkeys trying to hide, and giving you swigs of water when your voice becomes hoarse from all the shouting. Soon, the survivors have turned from a confused, desperate band into an efficient fighting force. Well done you!

You do so well that your attackers start to think twice. They're not used to this kind of resistance. Their prey is fighting back hard and they don't like it. Some of them turn tail and run.

Now's your chance. 'Everyone get to the walls!'

you shout. 'Give 'em everything you've got!'

Just as it looks like you're about to win, Scarlett says, 'Uh-oh. That's not good.'

She points out a large demon monkey getting ready to fling a huge fiery bundle at the watchtower where *you* are sitting. If it hits, you're going to be in a lot of trouble. Maybe you should get out of the tower while you still can? The survivors are winning now, so they might not need you to direct them any more.

Then again, perhaps you should stick at it. The demon monkey might miss, or one of the survivors might take him down.

To abandon the watchtower, head to page 127.

To stay at your post, head to page 92.

Sadly, your greed for gold unbalances you. Literally. Your extra weight at the back of the plane is too much, and the whole thing goes tumbling down into the ravine. Crispy explorer! Actually, it's more like crunchy explorer. Let's face it, falling into lava isn't going to leave you lightly toasted, is it? You're frizzled up like a firework! Probably best if we just move swiftly onward.

RUN AGAIN? TURN TO PAGE 10

A blast of flame engulfs you the second you step into the arch. Whoops. Looks like timing has nothing to do with it. There must be some other trick to getting through the Phoenix Gate. Maybe some future explorer will discover what it is. Unfortunately, your time on the volcanic island has come to a rather sudden end.

The legendary phoenix was able to rise again from the ashes. That would be a really useful trick to learn right now. All you seem to be able to do is sit there, crumbling softly in a little heap. What a way to go.

RUN AGAIN? TURN TO PAGE **10**

You take careful aim with your coconut, wind up your pitch, and throw.

It sails gracefully through the air, up . . . over . . . and down. It lands with a loud *clonk* right on the large demon monkey's skull.

The demon monkey drops the fireball he was about to throw. It rolls away down the beach, plunges into the sea and fizzles out.

For a moment, the demon monkey just stands there. You gulp. Any moment now he's going to charge the wall and probably smash right through it.

But no . . . his shoulders are jiggling up and down. He's covered his face with his claws. For such a big guy, he seems really upset. He can't be *crying*, can he?

Next thing you know, he's turned around and run away, heading back into the temple ruins. The monkey hordes don't seem to want to fight now that the big one has given up. They all follow him, giving up the attack.

Victory is yours, for now!

Head triumphantly to page 129.

Everything seems to go into slow motion. There's no time for you to climb down the rope ladder you used to get up here. All you can do is jump. You aim for the grass-thatched roof of a hut down below and pray it will break your fall.

The watchtower explodes in flame behind you. You land hard on the grass roof and go crashing down through the timbers.  You fall upside-down into the hut, dangling by one foot. A split second later, Scarlett falls through the roof too. The pair of you tumble to the ground with dry straw and fragments of wood showering down around you.

When you get your breath back, you say, 'I think we just trashed someone's house.'

'They can bill me,' Scarlett gasps. She gets to her feet and helps you stand. You can hardly believe you're still alive.

128

The watchtower is completely destroyed. Luckily, with your help, the survivors have already all but won the battle. Once they see you and Scarlett have survived, the demon monkeys give up in disgust. Victory is sweet!

Head triumphantly to page 129.

With the demon monkeys beaten for now, the survivors are a lot happier. They seem to think there's a real chance they might escape this island at last. But there's still one big problem. Hawk points up to the smoking volcano.

'Those flying rocks that sank our ships and nearly sank yours? It's not the volcano that's shooting 'em out. It's the gigantic demon monkey who lives in the volcano temple. The Island Guardian.'

Scarlett stares. 'I do hope you're joking.'

'I'm deadly serious, ma'am. He hurls boulders at any ship or aircraft that passes near the island. That's why so many have gone missing. We think he's protecting something precious. A mystery at the heart of the island.'

'So it wasn't the electromagnetic field causing the crashes at all. It was the Guardian!'

You chew over the problem. If you're going to make it safe for your ship to come close to land and rescue the survivors, you're going to have to reach the temple and deal with the giant Island Guardian one way or another.

'We need to get into the temple,' you tell Hawk. 'How do we get there?'

'There are two ways in,' Hawk says. 'You can go through the ruins or up the ceremonial ramp that the island people built, back in the old days.'

'The ruins are out,' Scarlett says. 'That's where the demon monkeys ran to when they gave up the attack. Let's check out the ramp.'

Hawk leads you to the ramp. It's nothing but a planked walkway held up by logs driven into the ground. It runs all the way from the beach, up the side of the volcano to a doorway right at the top. The bottom end, where you are, has completely collapsed.

'Gotta warn you, it's kind of flimsy and rickety,' Hawk warns you.

'You don't say,' Scarlett mutters. 'Have *you* ever climbed it?'

'Tried to,' Hawk says, sounding embarrassed and pointing to the broken section at the very start. 'It collapsed under my weight. We never did try again.'

You take a good look at that ramp. You don't weigh as much as a grown-up, so you might be able to climb it safely. Besides, you're quick and agile. You can easily jump from one part to another if it starts to collapse. The only question left is how you're going to get up there.

You ask Scarlett if she can help. With a grin, she produces a zipline launcher from her pack. 'I had a feeling we'd be needing this,' she comments. She fires a zipline up to the broken-off ramp and it latches on first time. You can use a hand-held motorised winch to get up, then just whizz back down when the time's right.

Scarlett hugs you. 'Good luck.'

It takes you moments to zoom up the zipline, climb on to the ramp and set off up to the volcano temple. The ramp creaks alarmingly under your weight, but you keep your balance. It's a good job you can go slowly. This would be a lot harder if you were running at speed, or being chased . . .

Eventually you reach the temple at the heart of the volcano.

Head straight on to page 133.

You realise you're getting close to the mystery at the heart of the island. You can just feel it. You move cautiously through a gigantic, open cavern towards a bright area in the distance. The air in here is sweltering. You blink sweat out of your eyes and try to focus.

Up ahead, you see the heart of the volcano temple. It's a chamber carved out of the rock, with an arched opening in the wall the size of a cathedral window. You realise the opening is carved out of the inside wall of the volcano. Through it you can see gobbets of lava spurting up into the air and dropping down again, like the most terrifying lava lamp ever created. You'd have a fantastic view of the boiling magma from there, but you'd risk falling in, too.

In front of the lava window is a pedestal with a golden idol sitting on it. You recognise the idol's fierce-looking expression from the other carvings in this temple. It's obviously an object of great power and value.

Suddenly you hear a snuffle and a roar from

somewhere close by. OK, so you've found the monstrous temple guardian, too. Try not to panic.

Right away you put out a call on the walkie-talkie, whispering in case the beast hears you. 'Scarlett? Barry? Karma? Anyone? You'll never believe what I'm looking at! It's an idol. A golden idol! This is the secret at the heart of the island. It has to be. This is what is being protected.'

Scarlett answers you excitedly. 'Then that's the key to getting the survivors off the island! Listen, our ship can't come close to land because of the giant demon monkey Guardian throwing rocks at it, OK? Well, he must be doing that to guard the idol, and prevent anyone coming to the island and taking it. So what you have to do is distract the Guardian for as long as you can, so he stops throwing boulders. Then we can evacuate the survivors!'

You can't believe what she's saying. 'Distract him? How am I meant to do that? Do a little dance?'

You hear Scarlett take a deep breath. 'You're going to have to steal the idol. The Island Guardian ought to pursue you when you do. That's what he's there for, after all. I know it's dangerous, and it's a lot to ask, but you're these people's only hope!'

You don't waste time thinking it over. If you did, you might lose your nerve. You run forward and grab the idol.

The volcano surges into life, and at the same time, a truly gigantic demon monkey stomps into the room, holding a huge boulder. He doesn't pause; he just flings it at you. You run for your life, followed by the demon monkey and by a rolling wave of lava flowing in through the arched window.

You flee through the cavern towards the two exits. One of them leads to the wooden ramp that runs around the outside of the volcano. The other leads to a balcony overlooking the ruined temple complex. You think you could jump down on to the rooftops without hurting yourself. You're going to have to choose which way to run.

To head down the wooden ramp, head to page 137.

To head to the balcony and jump down on to the rooftops, head to page 60.

The wooden ramp is terrifyingly unsafe with all this hot lava flying about. Sections burn away in front of you and you have to leap over sudden gaps. The Island Guardian pounds along behind you, roaring.

To your horror, the platform you're standing on cracks away from the volcano slope. If you jump as hard as you can, you might reach the next section of ramp, although you may have to dangle by your fingers. Or you could cling on to the swinging platform and try to jump for a tower you've spotted sticking up out of the ruins.

To jump for the next ramp section,
head to page 138.

To jump for the tower, head to page 79.

You go flying through the air and catch the wood of the ramp with one outstretched hand. It hurts like crazy, but you make it. You pull yourself up and keep going.

Behind you, the demon monkey roars in rage. You think he wanted you to fall. Now he has to jump the gap. His powerful legs mean he clears the jump easily, but he's a lot heavier than you. He lands hard, crashes through the ramp completely and has to struggle not to fall down into the ruins below.

While the Island Guardian pulls himself back up, buying you precious time, you keep running. There are smaller demon monkeys getting in on the act now. They've noticed you are carrying the idol and they mean to stop you. They come swarming up the ruined buildings below, heading for a tower high enough to jump from.

One of the small monkeys is getting ready to leap at you. You can either try to duck, in the hope it'll go flying over your head and slam into the side of the volcano, or you can try to smash it out of the air using the idol as a sort of bat. The idol's quite heavy, so you ought to be able to give the demon monkey quite a wallop.

To duck the demon monkey, go to page 141.

To knock it aside with the idol, go to page 76.

You try to push the gates shut, but the hinges are stiff after hundreds of years and they don't close quickly enough. Demon monkeys come pouring in through the gap. Looks like Karma doesn't always have the right idea.

With a dreadful screech, the horde surges forward as one. You and Karma hold them off for as long as you can, but eventually they bring you down. If you like, you can imagine the defeat happening in slow motion while a sad lady sings in the background, just like in an epic movie. You'll still be dead, but you might feel better about it.

RUN AGAIN? TURN TO PAGE **10**

You wait until the last possible moment. The demon monkey comes flying towards you in a frenzy of claws and teeth. You duck. It misses you completely, crashes into the mountainside and falls in a stunned heap. Serves it right!

You're almost at the bottom of the volcano now. But you're brought up short as you reach a huge section where the ramp has collapsed.

The huge Island Guardian is at your heels, and your hesitation is all he needs. He drops down in one bound and lunges for you. It looks like it's all over, but then there's a loud *twang* and a zipline shoots across the path, directly behind you. The monkey trips and falls, his gigantic skull ploughing up the sand. Scarlett Fox appears, zipline launcher in hand. 'That was a close one,' she grins.

While the monkey lies dazed, your friends hurry to load the survivors on to dinghies and ferry them out to the waiting ship.

Zip over to page 150.

'Erm . . . hello?' you say. The creature stares at you. You introduce yourself. When it answers back with Karma Lee's voice, you realise what's happening. The fumes from the volcano are giving you both hallucinations. You need to reach fresh air, and fast!

The pair of you run up the corridor to a tomb-like room. A waft of clean air reaches you from a crack in the wall. You both dive for it.

Head to page 77.

Vanderbolt is delighted with your advice. He says he'll stay. Barry grumbles, but there isn't a single thing he can do about it. There's nothing for it but for the two of you to head back to your dinghy.

Run to page 53.

Right at the edge of the rooftops, you come to a sudden halt. There's nowhere left to go. You've run out of roof, just as you feared you might. The Island Guardian is coming.

Next second, you feel wind in your face and hear the thunder of rotor blades. A helicopter appears over the jungle, heading your way. You recognise the people in the cockpit – Karma Lee, and an American explorer friend of hers, Guy Dangerous!

'Woohoo!' Guy bellows. 'The cavalry is here!'

'Thanks, Guy,' says Karma. 'That's another one I owe you.'

You leap and grab hold of the rope ladder they drop for you, while the Island Guardian rages and jumps up and down in fury. He jumps so hard he crashes down through the roof into the temple buildings. Now's your chance to evacuate the island!

Over the walkie-talkie, you stay in touch with Scarlett as she leads the evacuation operation. Guy Dangerous explains how he came to be in the area. His multimillionaire friend Zack Wonder has a

luxury yacht (complete with helicopter deck) that he takes on cruises from time to time. Zack and Guy got wind of Karma's expedition and thought they'd come along too, just in case.

'By the way,' Guy says, 'that idol you're carrying? I wouldn't hold on to it if I were you.'

Karma frowns. 'Surely it belongs in a museum?'

'Any other day I'd agree with you. But something tells me this one is more trouble than it's worth.'

You look down at the idol's staring eyes, and you realise Guy's right. As soon as Scarlett tells you that the last survivor has been evacuated, you ask Guy to fly you out over the sea. You throw the idol as hard as you can and watch it vanish beneath the blue waves.

Back in civilisation, your story makes the international news. The survivors are overjoyed to be reunited with their families. As for the island, it seems it sank without trace, along with all the demon monkeys. Maybe the idol called it home to the sea bed . . . who knows?

Well done! Your adventure has come to an

incredibly successful ending – but it's not the only one. Why not see what other secrets the volcanic island is keeping?

RUN AGAIN? TURN TO PAGE **10**

You grab the dish and drop it into the lava. Then you jump on, yelling – half from fear, half out of excitement.

Your crazy plan actually works! It's roasting hot, but the lava is flowing pretty fast and you manage to stay on your feet. The demon monkey bounds along behind you, but he clearly doesn't want to land in the lava if he can help it. That would be too much heat even for him.

You surf down through the survivors' huts on a wave of lava, holding the idol up like a sports trophy. You're exhausted and ready to collapse, but the demon monkey is still coming.

Barry Bones comes running over the beach. 'Kid, it's the idol he wants! Throw it over to me!'

You could throw the idol to Barry, but then you'd be putting him in danger. He looks pretty tired, too.

To throw the idol to Barry, head to page 78.

To hold on to it yourself, go to page 152.

Against all the odds, you manage to rescue all of the survivors, and round up everyone you came to the island with – Barry, Karma and Scarlett.

Not only that, you've got a spectacular golden idol to take back home. You plan to give it to a museum, but first, you're going to take one heck of a selfie with it. Congratulations, you're a hero! But the island does have other secrets, and you can't find them all on just one adventure . . .

RUN AGAIN? TURN TO PAGE **10**

You run down a sloping passageway as fast as your legs can carry you. Up ahead, filling the entire passage, is a monstrous frog the size of an elephant. Its eyes bulge and its throat sac balloons.

You realise this must be another illusion brought on by the choking fumes. A frog that huge can't possibly be real. You laugh as you run towards it. However, when a gigantic sticky tongue lashes out and ensnares you like a fly, you suddenly realise it's no illusion. This island is full of bizarre beasts, and you're about to be eaten by one of them. What a toad.

RUN AGAIN? TURN TO PAGE **10**

'Sorry, Barry. I need to take care of this myself!'
Barry nods and goes to help the survivors
escape to the ship. The Island Guardian chases you
up the beach. The survivors pelt him with coconuts,
but he ignores them. It's you he's after.

You're running out of breath, and you're running
out of places to run. The demon monkey seems
weary, too. The pair of you run up the beach, until
you see a terrible sight ahead of you.

A thick, glowing river of lava is blocking your
path. It's flowing all the way from the volcano down
to the beach, where it's solidifying on contact with
the water and sending up clouds of hissing steam.
There's nowhere left for you to go. You're caught
between the demon monkey and the lava.

The demon monkey sees you're trapped and slows
down. His fur is singed in many places. There's a
strange look on his bony face. Could it be ... respect?

He holds out a claw. He's not grabbing, or
snatching, or attacking. He's asking you for his idol
back.

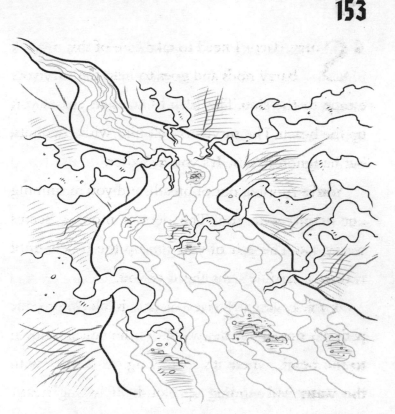

You know you can't give him the idol yet. There are still some survivors left to be rescued. There's only one thing to do.

You throw the golden idol into the lava.

The Guardian screams. The volcano lets loose a thunderous boom. Overhead, the skies go dark. You brace yourself and wait for those huge claws to strike you down.

But the blow never comes. The demon monkey's body freezes in place, in the moment of his greatest rage. A greyish colour creeps across his body. There's a soft crackling noise, like the sound of boots walking on dry mud, as he transforms. In seconds, the Island Guardian has turned completely to stone.

Stunned, you walk back across the beach. All across the landscape are tiny demon monkey statues, frozen in various poses. You know they were created only moments ago, but they already look impossibly old. Some of them are even crumbling to dust in front of you.

'What did you do?' Karma asks you, astonished.

'I . . . I don't know,' you tell her.

With the threat of the demon monkeys banished, you are able to evacuate all the remaining survivors safely. As you're sailing away, glad to leave the island behind you, there's a titanic rumbling sound

followed by a huge wave. The ship rocks madly and people have to cling on for dear life.

When you look again, the entire island is gone. There's no sign that it ever existed. Without the idol to prove your story, you may wonder in the days to come if this was all a crazy dream. At least you saved the shipwrecked people – that was real enough. Unless they, too, had the same bizarre dreams that you did. You don't suppose you'll ever know for sure.

Your story ends here . . . unless, of course, you'd like to see what other mysteries the volcanic island holds.

RUN AGAIN? TURN TO PAGE **10**